KU-633-882

The Children of
Noisy Village

Also by Astrid Lindgren

Pippi Longstocking
Pippi Longstocking Goes Aboard
Pippi Longstocking in the South Seas

The Children of Noisy Village
Happy Times in Noisy Village
Nothing But Fun in Noisy Village

Emil's Clever Pig
Emil and the Great Escape
Emil and the Sneaky Rat

Lotta Says 'No!'
Lotta Makes a Mess

Karlson on the Roof
Karlson Flies Again
The World's Best Karlson

The Brothers Lionheart
Ronia, the Robber's Daughter
Mio's Kingdom
Seacrow Island

The Children of Noisy Village

Astrid Lindgren

Translated by Susan Beard · Illustrated by Tony Ross

OXFORD
UNIVERSITY PRESS

OXFORD
UNIVERSITY PRESS

Great Clarendon Street, Oxford OX2 6DP

Oxford University Press is a department of the University of Oxford.
It furthers the University's objective of excellence in research, scholarship,
and education by publishing worldwide. Oxford is a registered trade mark of
Oxford University Press in the UK and in certain other countries

Text © Astrid Lindgren 1947, 2001 Saltkråkan AB
Illustrations © Tony Ross 2014

Translated from the Swedish by Susan Beard
English Translation © Susan Beard 2014

This translation of *The Children of Noisy Village* originally published in Swedish
published by arrangement with Saltkråkan Förvaltning AB

The moral rights of the author, illustrator, and translator have been asserted

First published as *Alla vi barn I Bullerbyn* by Rabén & Sjögren Bokförlag in 1947
This translation first published in the UK by Oxford University Press 2014

Database right Oxford University Press (maker)

All rights reserved. No part of this publication may be reproduced,
stored in a retrieval system, or transmitted, in any form or by any means,
without the prior permission in writing of Oxford University Press,
or as expressly permitted by law, or under terms agreed with the appropriate
reprographics rights organization. Enquiries concerning reproduction
outside the scope of the above should be sent to the Rights Department,
Oxford University Press, at the address above
You must not circulate this book in any other binding or cover
and you must impose this same condition on any acquirer

British Library Cataloguing in Publication Data
Data available

ISBN: 978-0-19-273459-4

7 9 10 8

Printed in Great Britain by Clays Ltd, St Ives plc

Paper used in the production of this book is a natural,
recyclable product made from wood grown in sustainable forests.
The manufacturing process conforms to the environmental
regulations of the country of origin.

CONTENTS

ALL OF US NOISY VILLAGE CHILDREN

My name is Lisa. I'm a girl. Well, you can tell that from the name, of course. I'm seven years old and I'll be eight soon. Sometimes Mum says:

'You're my big girl, so you can dry the dishes today.'

And sometimes Lasse and Bosse say:

'We don't let girls play Indians with us. Anyway, you're too little.'

That is why I wonder what I really am—big or little? When some people think you are big and some think you are little then perhaps you are just exactly the right age.

Lasse and Bosse are my brothers. Lasse is nine and Bosse is eight. Lasse is very strong and he can run much faster than me. But I can run as fast as Bosse. Sometimes, when Lasse and Bosse don't want me around, Lasse holds on to me while Bosse runs off and gets a head start. Then Lasse lets go of me and runs off as fast as anything. I haven't got a sister and that is a pity. Boys are so difficult.

The house where we live is called Middle Farmhouse. It is called that because it stands right between two other farmhouses. They are called North Farmhouse and South Farmhouse. All three houses are in a row, like this:

It doesn't look like that really, but I can't draw very well.

A boy called Olle lives in South Farmhouse. He hasn't got any brothers or sisters at all, but he plays with Lasse and Bosse. He is eight years old and he can run fast as well.

But there are girls at North Farm, two of them. What a good job they aren't boys as well! Their names are Britta and Anna. Britta is nine and Anna is the same age as me. I like them both just the same. Well, perhaps I like Anna a tiny, tiny bit more.

And that is all the children who live in Noisy Village. That is what it is called, our village. It is a very small village with only three houses: North Farmhouse, Middle Farmhouse, and South Farmhouse. And only six children: Lasse and Bosse and me, and Olle and Britta and Anna.

BROTHERS ARE DIFFICULT

Before, Lasse and Bosse and I shared the same room. It was the room on the right at the top of the house, at one end. Now I have the room on the left, which used to be Grandma's. But I'll tell you more about that later.

Sometimes it is lots of fun sharing a room with your brothers, but only sometimes. It was fun when we lay in bed at night telling ghost stories. Although it was scary, too. Lasse's ghost stories are so scary I had to hide under the quilt for a long, long time afterwards. Bosse never tells any ghost stories. All he talks about are the masses of adventures he is going to have when he grows up. He says he is going to live in America where the Indians are, and be an Indian chief.

One evening, after Lasse had told us a really horrible story about a ghost that went round a house moving all the furniture, I got so scared I thought I would die. It was practically pitch black in the room and my bed was such a long way from their beds, and guess what? All of a sudden a chair started jumping about, backwards and forwards. I thought the ghost had come to our house too, and was moving our furniture, and I screamed as loudly as I could. That's when I heard Lasse and Bosse giggling over in their beds. And do you know what? They had tied a piece of string to the chair and were lying in their beds pulling on the string and making the chair jump about. That was so typical of them. It made me angry at first, but then I couldn't help laughing.

Also, when you share a room with your brothers, and the brothers are bigger than you, you are never allowed to decide anything. It was always Lasse who decided when to turn out the light at night. When I wanted to lie in bed and read my *Our Sweden* magazine, Lasse wanted us to switch off the light and tell ghost stories. And if I was tired and wanted to go to sleep, then Lasse and Bosse wanted to play Snap. Lasse can lie in his bed and turn off the light whenever he wants because he stuck a piece of cardboard round the light switch with a piece of string tied to it. The string goes all the way to his bed. It is a very odd contraption and I can't really describe it properly because I'm not going to be a cog-spinning-sprocket-swashing-engineer when I grow up. That's what Lasse is going to be, he says. I don't know what a cog-spinning-sprocket-swashing-engineer is, but Lasse says it's something special and you have to know how to attach bits of cardboard to light switches if you are going to be one. Bosse is going to be an Indian chief. At least, that's what he always used to say. But the other day I heard him say that he was going to be a train driver, so perhaps he has changed his mind. I don't really know what I'm going to be. A mum, perhaps, because I like tiny little babies. I've got seven dolls and I'm their mummy. Soon I'll be too big to play with dolls. Oh no, how sad to be so grown up!

My best doll is called Bella. She has blue eyes and blonde curly hair. She sleeps in a doll's bed with a pink sheet and a cover that Mummy made. Once, when I went to pick Bella up out of her bed, she had a moustache and a little beard. Lasse and Bosse had drawn them on her with a black crayon. I'm glad I don't have to share their room any longer.

When you look out of the window in Lasse and Bosse's room you can see right into Olle's. His room is also on the side of the house, tucked under the roof. Middle Farmhouse and South Farmhouse are built awfully close together. It looks as if the houses are squashed up and jostling for space, Dad says. He thinks the people who first built the houses should have left a little more room between them. But Lasse, Bosse and Olle don't agree. They like it as it is.

There is a fence between Middle Farmhouse and South Farmhouse and halfway along the fence is an enormous tree. It is a linden tree, Dad says. Its branches reach all the way to Lasse and Bosse's window, and to Olle's window too. When Lasse and Bosse and Olle want to visit each other all they have to do is climb straight through the tree. That is much quicker than dashing down the stairs and out through the gate and then in through the next gate and up the stairs. Once our dad and Olle's dad decided to chop down the linden tree because it made the rooms so dark, but Lasse and Bosse and Olle nagged and nagged them to let it stay. And it was allowed to stay. It is still there today.

MY BEST BIRTHDAY EVER

I think my birthday and Christmas Eve are the best days of the whole year. My best birthday ever was when I was seven. This is what happened.

I woke up early. I was sharing Lasse and Bosse's room then. Lasse and Bosse were fast asleep in their beds. I have a bed that creaks, and I tossed and turned lots and lots of times so that it would creak a lot and wake them up. I couldn't call to them because when it is your birthday you have to pretend to be asleep until someone comes and wakes you up to wish you Happy Birthday. And there they were, fast asleep, instead of being busy with my waking-up celebration. I made that bed creak so much that finally Bosse sat up and scratched his head. Then he woke Lasse and they tiptoed out to the landing and down the stairs. I heard Mum rattling the coffee cups down in the kitchen and I was so excited I could hardly keep still.

At last I heard footsteps on the stairs and I closed my eyes as tight as I possibly could. And then, bang! The door flew open and there stood Dad and Mum and Lasse and Bosse and Agda, who helps Mum in the house. Mum was carrying the tray. On the tray was a cup of hot chocolate and a vase of flowers and a huge sponge cake with sugar and currants on the top and the words 'Lisa 7 years old' piped in icing. Agda had baked it. But there were no presents and I began to think this was a very odd kind of birthday. Then Dad said:

'Drink up your hot chocolate and we'll see if we can find some presents.'

Then I realized there was going to be a surprise and I gulped down the hot chocolate as fast as I could. Mum put a tea towel over my eyes as a blindfold, and

Dad spun me round and round and then he carried me somewhere. I had no idea where I was. I heard Lasse and Bosse running beside me, and I felt them too, because they kept pinching my toes and saying:

'Guess where you are!'

Dad carried me down the stairs and walked round and round, and after a while I felt I was out of doors. Then we went up some stairs again. Finally Mum took off the blindfold and we were in a room I had never seen before. At least, I thought I had never seen it, but then I decided to look out of the window and I saw the side of North Farmhouse next door. There in the window opposite stood Britta and Anna, waving at me. That was when I realized I was in Grandma's old room, and Dad had walked all that way to confuse me. Grandma lived with us when I was small, but a couple of years ago she moved to Auntie Frida's house. Since then Mum has kept her weaving loom in the room, with huge piles of rags in strips for making rugs. But now there was no weaving loom and there were no piles of rags. It was such a lovely, lovely room that I thought a magician must have been in there. Mum said it *was* a magician, and the magician was Dad, and he had magicked up a room for me which would be my very own, and that was my birthday present. I was so happy I screamed out loud, and I thought it was the best birthday present I had ever had. Dad said Mum had helped with the magic too. Dad had magicked up the wallpaper, such sweet paper with a mass of tiny, tiny sprigs of flowers, and Mum had magicked up curtains for the window. Dad had spent his evenings in the wood shed, magicking up a chest of drawers and a book shelf, and a round table and three chairs, and everything had been painted white. Mum had magicked up rag rugs, which were spread on the floor in stripes of red and yellow and green and black. I had seen them myself, when she was weaving them in the winter, but I certainly didn't think they were going to be for me. And I expect I had also seen Dad making the furniture, but Dad is always doing carpentry in the winter for people who can't make things themselves, so I had no idea at all that they were for me.

Immediately Lasse and Bosse struggled with my bed across the landing and into my new room. Lasse said:

'We'll come to your room in the evenings anyway, and tell ghost stories.'

The first thing I did was to run into Lasse and Bosse's room and fetch my dolls. I've got four small dolls and three big ones, because I have saved all the dolls I have been given ever since I was a little girl. I made a lovely room for the small dolls on a shelf. First I put down some red material for a carpet and on top of that I arranged the sweet little dolls' furniture I got from Grandma as a Christmas present, and then I put in the doll's beds, and lastly the small dolls themselves. Now they had their very own room, just like me, even though it wasn't their birthday. In a corner right next to my bed I stood the big doll's bed that Bella slept in. Then in another corner I put the doll's pram where Hans and Greta slept. Oh, how lovely it looked in my room!

Then I ran into Lasse and Bosse's room and fetched all my boxes and things that I kept in the chest of drawers, and Bosse said:

'Good! That means more room for my birds' eggs!'

I've got thirteen books that are my very own. I put them on a shelf too, along with all the *Our Sweden* magazines and my boxes of scraps. I've got so many scraps. We swap them at school. But I have twenty scraps that I will never, ever, give away. The best one is a big angel with a pink dress and wings. There was room for everything in my bookcase. It was so much fun, the day I was given my own room.

MORE FUN ON MY BIRTHDAY

I had even more fun that day. In the afternoon we had a party for all the Noisy Village children—only the six of us, that is. There was just enough room for all of us to sit round the table in my own room. We had raspberry squash and slices of the cake with 'Lisa 7 years old' written on the top, and two other kinds of cake that Agda had baked as well. I had presents from Britta and Anna and Olle. Britta and Anna gave me a storybook and Olle gave me a bar of chocolate. Olle sat next to me and then Lasse and Bosse started teasing us, saying:

'Boyfriend and girlfriend, boyfriend and girlfriend!'

They only say that because Olle isn't one of those stupid boys who never wants to play with girls. He doesn't care if they tease him, he plays with girls as well as boys anyway. Actually, Lasse and Bosse also want to play with girls, but they *pretend* they don't. When there are only six children in a village they have to play together, whether they are boys or girls. Practically every game is better when there are six of you and not just three.

After that the boys went to look at Bosse's birds' eggs, so Britta and I played with my dolls.

In my pocket I had a long, long piece of string. When I happened to feel it was there and pulled it out and saw how long it was, I thought we could have some fun with it. If we could find another piece that was the same length it would probably reach all the way to Britta and Anna's window in North Farmhouse. Then we could send letters to each other, in a cigar box. Oh, suddenly we couldn't wait to try it out! It worked. Britta and Anna ran back to their house and then we sat there for a long time, sending letters to each other. It was such fun seeing the cigar box glide along the string. At first we only wrote: 'How are you? I am well.' But then we pretended to be princesses who were trapped in two castles and couldn't get out because dragons were keeping guard, and Britta and Anna wrote to me: 'Our dragon is awfully scary. Is yours? Princess Britta and Princess Anna.'

And I replied: 'Yes, my dragon is awfully scary too. He bites me if I try to go outside. How lucky we can write to each other at least. Princess Lisa.'

After a while Mum called to me, saying I had to run an errand for her, and while I was gone Lasse and Bosse went into my room and happened to see the letters, so Lasse sent off a message in the cigar box. It said: 'Princess Lisa has gone to blow her nose but there is a heap of princes here. Prince Lars Alexander Napoleum.'

Britta and Anna thought that was stupid.

It is good, though, that my room faces North Farmhouse, because we often send letters to each other, Britta, Anna, and me. In the winter, when it's dark, it doesn't work so well, but then we flash our torches at each other instead. If I flash three times it means: 'Come here immediately! I've got something to tell you.'

Mum has told me that I have got to keep my room really neat and tidy. I try as hard as I can. Sometimes I have a big cleaning day. I throw all the mats out of the window and Agda helps me beat them. I've got a little carpet beater which is my very own and I use that to beat the mats. I polish the door handle and dust everywhere and put fresh flowers in the vase and make the doll's beds and tidy the doll's pram. Sometimes I forget to do the cleaning. Then Mum calls me Lazy-Lisa.

We Break Up for Summer

Summer is such fun. Everything is fun from the minute we break up for the holidays. I have only celebrated one special end of term day so far. It's like a test but it's fun too. The fun started already the evening before, when we decorated the classroom with flowers and leaves. All of us Noisy Village children collected silver birch branches and picked cowslips and almond blossom. We have to go a long way to get to school because it is in another village, called Storby Village. You can't have a school for only six children. The flowers had wilted a bit by the time we got there, but not much. As soon as they were put in water they became beautiful again. There were Swedish flags beside the blackboard and a garland of birch branches, and lots of flowers everywhere. The whole schoolroom was filled with a lovely scent.

When we had finished decorating we had to practise the songs we were going to sing on the special last day of term. They were *Hello, the Sunshine Calls to You*, and *Do You Think I am Lost and Forlorn For You Love Me No Longer*. One girl, called Ulla, sang it like this: 'Do you think I am lost on the lawn for you love me no longer.' She thought that was what the song said. How lucky our teacher had time to tell her what it really said, so she could sing it properly on the day!

It was such beautiful weather when we walked home afterwards. All of us Noisy Village children walked together. It took us a long time to get home. Lasse said we were only allowed to walk on the stones we saw along the roadside. It was game we played. We pretended that if you trod on the ground you would fall down dead. All of a sudden Olle stepped on the ground and Bosse said:

'Now you're dead!'

'No I'm not,' said Olle. 'Look how very alive I am.' And he wiggled his arms and legs. That made us laugh at him.

Then we balanced along the top of the fence. Lasse asked:

'Who decided we could only walk on the ground, do you think?'

Britta said she thought it must have been a grown-up.

'Highly likely,' said Lasse.

We walked on the fence for a long, long time, and it was such fun that I thought I would never walk on the road again. A man came along, riding on a milk wagon, and he said:

'Bless my soul, what can all those crows be doing on the fence?'

But the next day, when we were on our way to the last day of term, we couldn't walk on the fence because we were wearing our best clothes. I had on a brand new dress with red spots, and Britta and Anna were wearing blue dresses with frills. And we had new hair ribbons and new shoes.

There were a lot of parents sitting in the classroom, listening to us. I could answer all the questions the teacher asked me, but Bosse said 7 times 7 was 56. Then Lasse turned round and looked at him so sternly that Bosse said:

'No, course it isn't. I mean 46.'

In actual fact it's 49. I know that even though we haven't started doing multiplication tables yet, because I have heard the other children saying it. There are only twenty-three of us children in the school so we all sit together in one big classroom.

After we had sung all the songs we had learned, as well as the song we always sing at the end of the summer term, *Now all the Flowers are Blooming*, our teacher said:

'Goodbye everybody! Have a really wonderful summer!'

And then I felt something sort of jump inside me.

All of us Noisy Village children had good reports. We compared them on the way home. Actually, Bosse's marks weren't *that* good, but they were fairly good, anyway.

That evening we played rounders down by the

road. As we were playing the ball flew in among the blackcurrant bushes. I ran there to look for it, and guess what I found there? Tucked under a currant bush, right at the back, lay eleven eggs. That made me so happy. One of our hens is very contrary and she won't lay her eggs in the henhouse. She lays all her eggs out of doors. Lasse and Bosse and I have searched and searched to find where she lays them, but she is a cunning hen and very careful to make sure we don't see which way she goes. Mum said we could have five öre for every egg we find, and now I had found eggs worth 55 öre. But I didn't find the ball.

'We can use the eggs instead of a ball,' said Lasse. 'Then the whole of Noisy Village will be covered in scrambled egg.'

But I collected the eggs in my apron and took them into Mum and got 55 öre. I gave five öre to each child and put the rest in my piggy bank, which I lock with a tiny key. The key hangs on a nail at the back of the wardrobe.

Later, Anna found the ball, and we played rounders for hours. We went to bed much later than usual, but that didn't matter because it was the summer holidays and we could sleep as late as we liked the next morning.

We Thin Out the Turnips and Get a Kitten

I had even more money in my piggy bank later on, because I helped to thin out the turnip plants. We all did it, every child in Noisy Village. Of course, Lasse and Bosse and I should really have thinned out the turnips belonging to Middle Farm, and Britta and Anna the turnips belonging to North Farm, and Olle the ones belonging to South Farm, but instead we all helped each other with the turnips. We were paid for every row we thinned, 40 öre for the long ones and 20 öre for the very shortest.

We had aprons made from sacks to stop our knees hurting. Britta and Anna and I wore headscarves and looked like little old grannies, Mum said. We had a whole big jug of squash with us, in case we got thirsty. We got thirsty straight away and so we took long pieces of straw, stuck them into the jug, and then kneeled in a circle round the jug and drank. It was so much fun to suck the squash up through the straws that we drank and drank, until all of a sudden there was no squash left. Lasse picked up the jug and ran to the spring in the meadow next to our field and collected water for all of us, and so we drank water. It was as much fun as before, but not quite as tasty. Then Olle stretched out on the ground and said:

'Can you hear it sloshing around inside me?'

He had such a lot of water in his stomach and we all went over to him to hear it slosh about as he moved.

We chatted all the time while we were thinning the turnip plants, and told stories to each other. Lasse tried to tell ghost stories, but ghost stories are not scary when the sun is shining. Then, instead,

Lasse wanted us to have a competition to see who could swear the worst. But Britta and Anna and I didn't want to take part in that, because our teacher has said that only ignorant people swear. Lasse tried swearing a bit to himself, but it can't have gone very well because he soon stopped.

The first day we thinned out the turnip plants was the best. After that it got boring, but we had to carry on anyway because all the turnips had to be done.

Once, just after we had started for the day, Lasse said to Olle:

'Petruska saldo bumbum.'

And Olle said:

'Kollyfink, kollyfink.'

And Bosse said:

'Moysey doysey filliboom arrarat.'

We asked them what they were saying and Lasse told us it was a special language that only boys understood. It was far too difficult for girls, he said.

'Ha ha,' we laughed. 'You don't even understand it yourselves!'

'Yes we do,' said Lasse. 'What I said first meant "It's a beautiful day", and then Olle answered "Yes it is, yes it is", and then Bosse said "Good job the girls don't understand".'

Then they talked in their language in long, long strings of words, until Britta said we had a language too, that only girls understood, and we started speaking our language. And so we lay in the turnip field talking in our different languages all morning. I couldn't actually hear any difference in the languages, but Lasse said ours was silly. The boys' language was much better, he said, because it was almost like Russian.

'Kollyfink, kollyfink,' said Olle again. We had learned enough of the boys' language to know that meant "Yes, it is, yes it is". And now Britta and Anna and I never call Olle anything else except Olle Kollyfink.

One afternoon, while we were doing the turnip thinning, we had just sat down on a pile of rocks to drink our hot chocolate and eat our sandwiches, which we had packed for lunch, when the sky came over all dark and a terrible thunderstorm began. There was hail, too. There was so much hail it piled up in drifts, just like in the winter. We started running. We were barefoot and our feet froze as we ran through the drifts of hail.

'Let's run to Kristin in Lövnäset,' Lasse said. We nearly always do what Lasse says, and so that's what we did this time as well. Kristin lived in a little red cottage not far away. We ran there and luckily Kristin was home. Kristin is a very old woman. She looks like a granny, more or less. And she is so kind. I have been to her house many times.

'Oh goodness gracious me,' she said, clapping her hands together. And then she said: 'Oh dear, oh dear, you poor little mites!'

She lit a big fire in the fireplace in her sitting room, and we took off our wet clothes and warmed our feet in front of the fire. Then she toasted bread for us on a long fork which she held over the burning wood. She made coffee for us too, in a coffee pot which stood on three legs in the middle of the fire.

Kristin has three cats and one of them had recently had kittens. They were in a basket and they were mewing and were so sweet. There were four of them and Kristin told us she had to give them all away, except one, because otherwise she would have a house full of cats and there would be no room for her to live there.

'Oh, can't we have them?' shrieked Anna.

Kristin said yes, of course we could, but she wasn't sure our mums would like it if we came home with kittens.

'But everyone likes kittens, don't they?' Britta said.

We pleaded and begged to take them home, just to see if we could keep them. And do you know what? There were exactly enough kittens for one to go to North Farmhouse, one to Middle Farmhouse, and one to South Farmhouse. Lasse picked out the one we were going to have, a little tabby kitten with a white patch on its forehead. Britta and Anna had one that was completely white, and Olle had a black one.

When our clothes were dry we walked home with our kittens. I'm glad the cat mummy could keep one of her kittens, otherwise she wouldn't have had any children.

We called our kitten Milo, Britta and Anna called theirs Sessan, and Olle called his Malkolm. None of our mums minded that we brought the kittens home—we *were* allowed to keep them.

I played such a lot with Milo. I tied a piece of paper to the end of a piece of string and ran around with it, and Milo ran after me, trying to catch it. Lasse and Bosse also played with him to start with, but they soon lost interest in him.

It was me who made sure he had food. He drank milk from a saucer in the kitchen. He didn't drink the way people do. Instead he stuck out his tongue, which was all pink, and lapped up the milk. I prepared a basket for him to sleep in, and I made it so soft and cosy. Sometimes we let Milo and Sessan and Malkolm out onto the grass, so they could play. They were from the same family after all, so I'm sure they wanted to be together.

I earned nine kronor and 40 öre from thinning out the turnip plants, and I put all of it into my piggy bank because I'm saving for a bicycle. A red bicycle.

How Olle Got His Dog

Olle hasn't got any brothers or sisters, but he's got a dog. And Malkolm, of course. The dog is called Svipp. Now I'm going to tell you what happened when Olle got Svipp, exactly the way he told us.

Between Noisy Village and Storby Village is the shoemaker's cottage, and that is where Mr Gentle lives. He is *called* Mr Gentle but he isn't gentle, not in the slightest. He never has our shoes ready for us when we go to collect them, even if he has promised again and again that they will be. It is because he drinks so much, says Agda. He was the person who owned Svipp before Olle. He was never kind to Svipp, and Svipp was the fiercest dog for miles around. He was always chained to his dog kennel and every time you went to take shoes to Mr Gentle, Svipp would rush out of his kennel, barking. We were so afraid of him we never dared go near. We were afraid of the shoemaker too, because he was always so bad tempered and used to say: 'Kids are nothing but a load of trouble and should be beaten every day.' Svipp was beaten too, a lot, even though he was a dog and not a kid. Perhaps Mr Gentle thought dogs should be beaten every day too. When Mr Gentle was drunk he forgot to give Svipp any food.

While Svipp was living with the shoemaker I used to think he was a nasty, ugly dog. His coat was dirty and tangled, and he growled and barked all the time. Now I think he is a gentle, beautiful dog. Olle is the one who has made him gentle. Olle is so gentle himself.

Once, when Olle went to the shoemaker's with his shoes and Svipp came rushing out as usual, barking at him and looking as if he would bite him,

Olle stopped and talked to him and said he was a good dog and that he shouldn't bark like that. He stood at a distance, of course, so that Svipp couldn't reach him. Svipp looked as angry as he always did and behaved as if he wasn't a good dog at all.

When Olle came to collect his shoes he had a meaty bone with him for Svipp. Svipp barked and growled, but he was so hungry he grabbed the bone between his teeth. All the time Svipp was eating Olle stood a little bit away from him, telling him what a lovely, good dog he was.

Olle had to go and ask for his shoes many times, I can tell you, because they were never ready, and every time he went he took something tasty for Svipp. Then one fine day, guess what? Svipp didn't growl at him any more, but only barked in that kind of way dogs do when they see someone they like. So Olle walked up to Svipp and patted him, and Svipp licked his hand.

Then one day the shoemaker tripped over and sprained his ankle, and he couldn't be bothered if Svipp got any food or not. Olle felt very sorry for Svipp, and that is why he went to Mr Gentle and asked if he could look after Svipp while Mr Gentle's ankle was getting better. To think that he dared! But Mr Gentle said:

'Ha, that would be worth seeing! He'll go straight for your throat the minute you get near him.'

But Olle went out to Svipp and stroked him, and the shoemaker stood in window, watching. That's when he said Olle could look after Svipp for a little while, because he couldn't do it himself.

Olle made Svipp's kennel so nice inside. He put down clean straw and then he washed out his water bowl and filled it with fresh water. He gave him plenty of food, too. Then he took him on a long walk all the way home to Noisy Village, and Svipp yelped and jumped for joy because he had been tied up for such a long time and he was very fed up with it. Every day, for as long as Mr Gentle's ankle was getting better, Olle fetched Svipp and took him out for a run. We ran with him as well, but Svipp likes Olle best and no one else was allowed to hold the lead otherwise Svipp growled.

But when the shoemaker's ankle was better, he said to Olle:

'That's enough of this nonsense. The mongrel's a guard dog and he's got to go back in his kennel.'

Svipp thought he was going to go for a walk with Olle as usual, and he jumped and yelped, but when Olle walked off without him he whined and sounded very sad, Olle said. And Olle was sad for many days until eventually his dad didn't want to see him looking sad any more, and he went to Mr Gentle and bought Svipp for Olle. And all of us Noisy Village children went to Olle's house and watched as Olle gave Svipp a bath in the outhouse where they did their washing. We helped a bit. After Svipp had been bathed and dried and combed, he was a different dog altogether.

And these days he is never angry and never has to walk on a lead. He sleeps under Olle's bed every night, and when all of us Noisy Village children walk home from school, Svipp meets Olle halfway and carries his school bag. But he never goes as far as Mr Gentle's cottage. Perhaps he is afraid that Mr Gentle will come out and take him.

IT'S FUN HAVING YOUR OWN PET
BUT A GRANDAD IS ALSO GOOD

It's fun having your very own pet. I would also like to have a dog, but I haven't got one. We have so many animals here in Noisy Village, horses and cows and calves and pigs and sheep. And Mum has masses of hens. It's called Noisy Village Hatchery and Mum sends eggs all over the place to people who want chickens. One of our horses, called Ajax, belongs to me, but he isn't really, really mine the same way that Svipp is Olle's. But I do have rabbits that are really mine. They live in a run that Dad made for me, and every day I have to go and give them grass and dandelion leaves. When winter comes I move the run into the barn. They have lots of babies and I have sold masses to Bosse and Olle. Bosse had rabbits for a time, but he got bored with them because he gets bored with everything except his birds' eggs.*

In our garden is an old tree which we call Owl Tree because owls live in it. Once Bosse climbed up into Owl Tree and took one of the owl's eggs. There were four eggs in the nest, so at least the owl had three left. Bosse blew out the insides of the egg and put it in a drawer along with his other birds' eggs. Then he thought he would play a joke on the owl mother, so he climbed up to the nest and put a hen's egg in there instead. How strange that the owl mother never noticed the difference! She really didn't. She continued to sit on the eggs and then one day there were three owl babies and one chick in the nest. The owl mother must have been very surprised when she noticed that one of her babies looked like a tiny yellow ball! Bosse was afraid the owl mother wouldn't like the chick, so he took it away.

* See back of book for note about birds' eggs.

'It's my chick, anyway,' he said.

He tied a piece of red thread around the chick's leg so that he would recognize it, and then he let it go among Mum's other chicks. He called it Albert, but when Albert grew a bit older it turned out to be a little hen and not a cockerel after all, so Bosse called it Albertina. And now Albertina is a big hen, and every time Bosse eats an egg he says:

'I expect Albertina laid this egg for me.'

Albertina flaps and flies more than any of the other hens. That is probably because she was born in an owl's nest, Bosse says.

Once Lasse thought he would also like some animals of his own. That is why he put three traps in the pigsty and caught sixteen big field voles which he shut inside a barrel. He painted a large sign and stuck it on the barrel. Noisy Village Vole Hatchery, the sign said. But during the night the voles escaped from the barrel, so that was the end of that vole hatchery.

'What did you want a vole hatchery for, anyway?' asked Britta. 'Voles don't lay eggs.'

'I just think it would have been fun, can't you see

that?' answered Lasse, who was angry because the voles had escaped.

Britta and Anna haven't got a dog, and no rabbits either. In fact they haven't got any animals of their own at all. But they do have a grandad. He is the kindest grandad in the whole wide world, that's for sure. All of us Noisy Village children call him Grandad, even though he isn't Grandad to all of us, only to Britta and Anna. He lives in a room on the top floor of North Farmhouse. It is such a nice room with such a nice Grandad, and all of us children go there when we are not busy doing anything else. Grandad sits in a rocking chair and he has a long, long white beard just like Father Christmas. His eyes are so bad that he can hardly see anything. He can't read any books or newspapers, but that doesn't matter because he knows everything the books say anyway. He tells us Bible stories and what it was like in the old days, when he was a little boy. We read the paper to him, Britta and Anna and me, all about everyone who has died or has a special birthday, and all the accidents and advertisements and everything. If it says in the paper that lightning has struck somewhere, then Grandad knows at least twenty places where lightning struck in the old days. And if it says someone has been gored to death by a bull, then Grandad tells us about all the people he has known who have been attacked by an angry bull. That means it can take quite a long time before we have finished reading the whole newspaper. The boys read to him sometimes, but he prefers it when Britta and Anna and I do it because the boys rush through it, missing out some of the advertisements and things like that. Grandad has a tool box in his wardrobe which he lets the boys use, and he helps them to carve boats, even though he can't see. And when the boys want to make tin soldiers, they always go to Grandad and heat the lead in in his stove.

Inside his wardrobe Grandad always keeps a box of apples—well, not always, of course, only when it's that time of year—so there are apples for us to eat. Every time we go to see him we get an apple. We have to buy him barley sugar from Storby Village, and he keeps it in a bag in the corner cupboard in his room. So we get both barley sugar and apples from him.

Grandad has geraniums on his window sill and he looks after them well, even though he is almost blind. He talks to them for ages. On the walls in Grandad's room are beautiful pictures. There are two I like especially. One of them shows Jonas inside the whale's stomach and the other is a snake that has escaped from a zoo and is squeezing a man to death. It is not beautiful, exactly, but it is scary and exciting.

When the weather is good Grandad goes out walking. He has a stick and he feels his way along with it. In the summer he mainly sits under the big elm tree in the middle of the grass right in front of North Farmhouse. He sits there, warming himself in the sun, and from time to time he chuckles:

'Heh, heh, heh!'

We have asked him why he says 'Heh, heh, heh,' and Grandad says it is because he is thinking of when he was young. That must have been a very long time ago, I think. But imagine having such a lovely Grandad! I like him so much. I would much rather have him than a dog.

BOYS CAN'T HAVE SECRETS

After we had finished thinning out the turnips there weren't many days left until haymaking began.

'This year I don't want any youngsters up in the hayloft, trampling all over the hay,' said Dad. He says that every year but no one thinks he means it.

All day we rode on the hay carts and jumped on the hay in hayloft. Lasse wanted us to have a competition to see who could jump the highest— down from the top, of course, not up from the bottom. We climbed on the beams under the roof and then jumped down onto the hay below. Ooh, it gave me butterflies in my stomach! Lasse said that whoever won the competition would get a lollipop as a prize. He had bought it that day when he was in the shop in Storby Village, buying yeast for Mum. So we jumped and jumped, trying to beat each other, but in the end Lasse climbed up as high as he could and then jumped down onto a tiny, tiny flat pile of hay. He bounced and then lay still for a long time, unable to move. Afterwards he told us that he thought his heart had dropped into his stomach and that he would be walking around with it there for as long as he lived. Nobody else dared to do that jump, and so Lasse put the lollipop in his mouth and said:

'Presented to Lars for heroic deeds in the hayloft!' Lars is Lasse's real name.

One day, while Britta and Anna and I were riding on the hay cart driven by the farmhand from North Farm, we came across a patch of wild strawberries on a rocky slope in the field where we were collecting hay. There were so many wild strawberries growing there, more than I had ever seen before. We agreed we would never, ever, ever tell anyone about that wild strawberry patch, not the boys or anyone else.

We picked wild strawberries and threaded them onto long stalks of hay and we got thirteen stalks full. That evening we ate them with sugar and cream. We let Lasse and Bosse and Olle taste a couple each, but when they wanted to know where we had picked the strawberries we said:

'We'll never say because it's a secret.'

After that Britta and Anna and I ran around for several days looking for more wild strawberry patches, and we didn't care about the hayloft. But the boys were there, and we couldn't understand why they never grew tired of it.

One day we found so many strawberries that we told the boys we now had seven wild strawberry patches we were never going to tell them about, because they were a secret. Then Olle said:

'Ha ha, that's a useless secret compared to ours!'

'What's your secret?' asked Britta.

'Don't tell, Lasse,' said Olle.

But Lasse said:

'Yes, I will tell! Just so they know our secret isn't as stupid as theirs.'

'What is it, then?' we asked.

'We have made nine caves in the hay, if you really want to know,' answered Lasse.

'But we're not saying where,' said Bosse, hopping on one leg.

'We'll soon find them,' we said, and we raced off to our hayloft to look. We looked all that day and the one after that, but we didn't find any caves. The boys were acting as if they were so important, and Lasse said:

'You'll never find them! For one thing they can't be found without a map, and for another you'll never find the map that tells you where they are.'

'What map is that?' we asked.

'The map we made,' replied Lasse. 'But we have hidden it.'

So Britta and Anna and I started looking for the map instead. We thought it was sure to be somewhere in Middle Farmhouse, because Lasse probably wouldn't agree to hiding it anywhere else. We searched in Lasse and Bosse's room for hours, in their beds and their drawers and in the wardrobe and everywhere. Then we said to Lasse:

'You can at least say if it's bird or fish or in between.'

That's what you say, when you play hunt the thimble.

Then Lasse and Bosse and Olle laughed their heads off, and Lasse said:

'It's bird! You can definitely say it's bird!'

And they winked and looked secretively at each other. We searched in the lampshade and looked to see if there was a map stuffed behind the wallpaper up by the ceiling, but Lasse said:

'You might as well give up because you'll never find the map anyway.'

So we didn't bother about it any longer. But the next day I thought I'd ask Olle if I could borrow his *Thousand and One Nights* storybook because it was raining and I wanted to stay indoors and read. Lasse and Bosse were out, and I went into their room to climb across the linden tree to Olle's.

There had been a little bird living in the tree before, and a hole went deep into the tree trunk where his nest had been. He didn't live there any more, but when I climbed past his nest I could see a piece of string poking out of it.

'What on earth did the bird want a piece of string for?' I thought, and I pulled it out. There was a roll of paper tied to one end and you'll never believe this, but it was the map! I thought I was going to fall right out of the tree, I was so surprised. I forgot *A Thousand and One Nights* and climbed back into Lasse and Bosse's room and ran to find Britta and Anna as fast as I could. I was in such a hurry that I tripped on the stairs and banged my knee.

Oh, how happy Britta and Anna were! Then we were in a mad rush to get to the hayloft, and it wasn't long before we had found all the caves. The boys had made long passages among the hay bales and they were all there, marked on the map. When you crawl along one of those passages and it is so dark and you are surrounded by so much hay, you can't help thinking:

'What if I can never get out again?'

It feels awful and very exciting. But you always do get out again.

It was dark in the passages. In the caves it was light, because they were all up against the wall and light was coming in through the cracks. They were lovely big caves, and we realized the boys must have worked terribly hard to make them. The passage to the last cave was so very, very long that we thought it would never come to an end. I crawled in front, followed by Britta and then Anna.

'We're in a never-ending labyrinth, you wait and see,' said Britta.

But just as she said that I noticed it was getting lighter ahead, and there was the cave. And do you know what? There sat Lasse and Bosse and Olle! They were *very* surprised when we stuck our noses into their cave!

'How did you find us?' asked Lasse.

'Ha ha, we found the map, of course!' I said. 'It wasn't difficult. Such an easy hiding place!'

For once Lasse looked confused, but after thinking for a while he said:

'Fine by me! The girls can join in!'

Then we played all day in the caves while the rain fell outside, and we had so much fun. But the next day Lasse said:

'Now you know our secret, it's only fair you tell us about your wild strawberry patches.'

'That's what you think,' we said. 'You can find them yourselves, just like we found out where the caves were.'

But to make it easier, Britta and Anna and I laid out arrows made of sticks on the ground, although the arrows were so far apart it was a long time before the boys found the wild strawberry patches. We didn't show the way to our very best wild strawberry patches. That is our secret and we will never, ever, ever tell anyone.

WE SLEEP IN THE HAYLOFT

One day Bosse said to me:

'Lasse and I are going to sleep in the hayloft tonight. And Olle too, if he's allowed.'

'It's only tramps who sleep in haylofts,' I said.

'No it isn't,' Bosse said. 'We've asked Mum and we're allowed.'

I ran and told Britta and Anna.

'Then we'll sleep in our hayloft,' they said. 'You too, Lisa.'

So that's what we decided to do. Ooh, what fun it was going to be! It was annoying that the boys had thought of it first, though, and not us. I ran home to Mum straight away to ask if I could, and she said yes. Mum didn't think little girls ought to be sleeping in haylofts, but I told her girls had to have fun too, not only boys, so I was allowed.

We could hardly wait for it to be evening. Lasse said:

'Are you girls going to sleep in the barn too? You won't dare! What if a ghost appears?'

'Of course we dare!' we said, and we made sandwiches for ourselves in case we felt hungry during the night. And then the boys also made sandwiches.

We set off at eight o'clock that night, the boys to Middle Farm's hayloft and us to North Farm's. We had a horse blanket each. Olle Kollyfink took Svipp with him. Lucky thing, to have a dog!

'Good night, little tramps,' Dad said. And Mum said:

'You'll come in tomorrow and buy milk, won't you? That's what tramps do.'

When we said goodnight to the boys Lasse said:

'Sleep well, if you can! Last year they found a

poisonous snake in the hay in North Farm's hayloft. I wonder if there's one there this year?'

And Bosse said:

'Maybe, maybe not. But I bet there'll be loads of field voles. Ugh, nasty!'

'Ah, poor little things,' we said. 'Are you afraid of field voles? Then it's best you go home and sleep in your own beds.'

Then we left, with our blankets and our sandwiches. It was light outside but up in the hayloft it is almost always dark.

'Bags I lie in the middle!' I shouted.

Then we made a bed for ourselves in the hay. It smelled good, but it prickled, though once we had wrapped ourselves in our blankets we were really comfy.

We lay there talking and wondering what it must be like to be a real tramp who always slept in barns. Anna said she thought it would be nice. We weren't at all tired, just hungry. So we thought we might as well eat our sandwiches before it got too dark. Finally it grew so dark around us that we couldn't see our hands when we held them up in front of our faces. I was very glad I was lying between Britta and Anna. There was a strange rustling in the hay. Britta and Anna wriggled closer to me.

'What if a real tramp comes in here to sleep,' whispered Britta. 'Without asking permission?'

We lay in silence for a while, thinking about that. And then, all of a sudden there was a wail. A horrible, terrifying wail! It sounded as if a thousand ghosts had started wailing all at the same time. We nearly died! We didn't, but we screamed. And oh, how Lasse and Bosse and Olle laughed!

Because it was them who had been doing the wailing. And of course it was them making the hay rustle as they crawled closer. Britta said it was dangerous to frighten people because the blood could freeze solid in their veins, and she was going to tell her mum. Then Lasse said:

'But we were only having fun!' And Bosse said:

'Telltale! Telltale!'

Anna said she felt as if the blood had frozen in her veins, just a little bit.

Eventually the boys went back to their hayloft. We wondered if we should creep into their hayloft and scare them too, but we couldn't because we were too sleepy.

We were woken by the cockerel crowing at North Farm, and because we were cold. Brrr, it was so cold! We didn't know what the time was, but we thought it was probably time to get up. And just as we stuck our noses out of the barn door, Lasse and Bosse and Olle came out from Middle Farm's hayloft. They were cold too. We ran into my kitchen to warm up, and do you know what? No one was awake! They were all asleep because it was only half past four. But soon we heard Agda's alarm clock. She had to get up to milk the cows. She gave all of us warm milk and cinnamon buns. Oh, they were so delicious!

Afterwards I hurried upstairs to snuggle down in my own bed, because I wanted to go back to sleep. The person who invented beds must have been very wise because you actually sleep much better in your bed than in the hayloft.

WHEN ANNA AND I WERE
GOING TO RUN AWAY

I don't think anyone is as much fun to play with as Anna. We have so many let's-pretend games that only she and I know. Sometimes we pretend we are two ladies who visit each other. Then Anna is called Mrs Bengtsson and I am called Mrs Larsson. Anna looks so posh when she is Mrs Bengtsson, and she speaks very posh too. I speak posh as well when I am Mrs Larsson. Sometimes we pretend that Mrs Bengtsson and Mrs Larsson quarrel, and then Anna says:

'In that case Mrs Larsson can go home and take her revolting children with her!'

It's my dolls she is calling 'revolting children'. So I always say:

'I think Mrs Larsson's children are the ones who are revolting!'

But then we make friends again and pretend to go to the shops and buy silk and velvet and sweets. We have pretend money that we make ourselves up at Grandad's. We are so scared that Lasse and the others will hear us when we are playing pretend because they laugh at us. It doesn't matter if Grandad hears because he pretends himself sometimes, and we buy things from him with our pretend money.

When it rains Anna and I often sit with Grandad and read the newspaper to him. When Grandad was a little boy his mum and dad died and left him alone, and he had to go to other people who weren't kind to him at all. He had to work very hard even though he was so young, and he had so many beatings and hardly any food that finally he got fed up and ran away. Then he had so many exciting adventures you'd never believe it, until he found some nice people he was allowed to stay with.

One rainy day when Anna and I were with Grandad and had finished reading the paper, Anna said:

'Grandad, tell us about when you ran away.'

'Deary, deary me,' said Grandad. 'You have heard that so many times before.'

But we nagged him to tell us again, and so he did. When he had finished Anna said:

'It must be fun to run away. I could think of doing that myself.'

'Yes, but you've got to have cruel people to run away from first,' I said.

'No, you haven't!' Anna said. 'You can run away in any case. For a little while. And come back later.'

'Oh yes! Let's do that,' I said.

'What do you say, Grandad?' Anna asked him. 'Do you think we could?'

And Grandad said why not, we could run away a little bit. And so we decided that was what we would do. It had to happen at night, of course, and no one else would know about it. We told Grandad that he was not allowed to tell anyone. He promised he wouldn't.

I always find it very hard to stay awake in the evenings, so I had no idea how I was going to stop myself from falling asleep before it was time to run away. But then Anna said:

'It's all right, you go to sleep! We'll tie a piece of string around your big toe and hang the other end out of the window. Then I'll come and pull on it and you'll wake up.'

Anna said she was going to pick some prickly branches to put in her bed, and she thought that would probably keep her awake until after everyone else had fallen asleep.

Then we asked Grandad what people ought to take with them when they ran away, and he said you needed some food and perhaps a little money, if you had some. We planned to run away that very night so we were kept busy getting everything ready. I went to Mum and asked for some sandwiches, and she said:

'Are you hungry again already? We've only just eaten dinner.'

Now, I couldn't tell her why we wanted the sandwiches, so I didn't answer. Then I took a few kronor from my turnip-thinning money and put them under my pillow. After that I went to look for a long piece of string to tie around my big toe.

That evening we played rounders, all of us children together, and when at last it was time to go to bed, Anna and I winked at each other and whispered:

'Half past ten!'

I hugged Mum and Dad so hard when I said goodnight, because I thought that I wouldn't be seeing them for quite a long time. And when Mum said: 'Let's pick blackcurrants tomorrow, you and me,' I felt so dreadfully sorry for her because she wouldn't have a daughter tomorrow.

Then I went upstairs to my room, tied the string around my big toe and dropped the other end out of the window. Then I got into bed and thought I ought to hurry up and fall asleep for a little while so that I wouldn't be tired when it was time to run away.

Usually I fall asleep as soon as my head touches the pillow, but it wouldn't work this time. I tried as hard as I could but as soon as I moved, the string pulled on my big toe. And then I thought about what Mum would say when she came into my room next morning and saw my empty bed. I felt so sorry for her that I started to cry. I cried for a long, long time.

All of a sudden I woke up. My big toe felt so strange and at first I couldn't understand what it was. But then I remembered. Someone was pulling the string.

'All right, Anna, I'm coming!' I called, and I leapt out of bed and ran to the window. It was broad daylight. And there was Lasse, standing underneath my window, tugging on the string. Oh, I was so angry!

'Ow! Ow!' I shouted. 'Stop doing that!'

But Lasse kept tugging.

'Stop it!' I shouted.

'Why?' asked Lasse.

'Because the string is tied to my big toe,' I yelled.

Then Lasse laughed and said:

'Well, well, what a very strange fish I've caught on the end of my line!'

Then he wanted to know what the string was for, but I didn't stay to tell him. Instead I ran to North Farmhouse. I thought perhaps Anna had run away alone. Britta was sitting on the steps playing with Sessan.

'Where's Anna?' I asked her.

'Asleep,' Britta answered.

So I went up to their room, and there she was, asleep. And snoring. I tried to tie the string around her big toe, but she woke up.

'Oh,' she said. 'What's the time?'

And when I told her it was eight o'clock in the morning she sat there in complete silence for a few moments. Then she said:

'All those people who can't sleep at night should try sleeping on pine tree branches. You won't believe how sleepy it makes you.'

Then we went to Grandad to read the paper, and when we went skipping into his room he was so startled that he said:

'What's this? Haven't you run away?'

'Another time,' we said.

WE PLAY HOUSE

Eventually we grew tired of playing in the hay. Lasse and Bosse and Olle disappeared every morning. We didn't know where, and we didn't care either, because we were having fun ourselves. In the meadow behind South Farmhouse there are lots of lovely little rocky slopes. That's where we played, me and Britta and Anna. One day Britta came up with the idea of making a house in a crevice among the rocks. It was just like a little room inside.

Oh, we had fun! It was such a brilliant pretend house, the best we had ever made. I asked Mum if we were allowed to have a few small rag rugs, and we were. We spread them over the flat rock and that made it look even more like a room. Then we used crates for cupboards and stood them here and there, and we put a square box in the middle as a table. Britta borrowed a check headscarf from her mum to use as a tablecloth. And we each brought our own little stool to sit on. I also brought along my beautiful dolls' tea set, which is pink, and Anna fetched her little glass jug with flowers on, with matching glasses. We put everything in the crates, but only after we had covered the bottom with shelf paper, of course. Then we went and picked masses of harebells and daisies and put them in the middle of the table in a jam jar filled with water. Oh, how pretty it all looked!

Agda was baking that day so we baked too, making tiny weeny buns for the dolls. Then we sat round the table in our pretend house, drinking coffee from my pink tea set and eating the buns. Anna went and fetched squash in her jug, so we drank squash too.

We played that it was Britta's house and she was called Mrs Andersson, and I was the maid, called Agda, and Anna was the child. We picked raspberries that were growing nearby and squeezed them in a bit of white cloth and pretended we were making cheese. Britta, who was Mrs Andersson, said to me:

'To *think* that Agda can never learn to make cheese properly!'

And I said:

'Mrs Andersson can make her rotten cheese herself.'

Just as I said that I caught sight of Bosse's fringe peeping out from behind a big rock, and I said to Britta and Anna:

'The boys are spying on us.'

And so we yelled:

'Ha! We've seen you so you might as well come out.'

And out jumped Lasse and Bosse and Olle, and they were so idiotic they copied us, shouting:

'To *think* that Agda can never make Mrs Andersson's rotten cheese properly!'

They wouldn't leave us alone, so we couldn't play any more that day. Lasse wanted us to play rounders, so we did. But Lasse was still being silly because he said:

'To *think* that Mrs Andersson can't sprint a little faster! Watch out for the ball, Mrs Andersson!'

JUST LIKE I SAID—BOYS CAN'T HAVE SECRETS

The very next morning Lasse and Bosse and Olle disappeared again as soon as they had eaten their porridge. And when Britta and Anna and I had played in our make believe house all morning and didn't want to play house any longer, we began to wonder what the boys were actually doing and where they were spending their days. We hadn't thought about it before, but now we realized we had hardly seen them for a whole week, apart from the evenings when we played rounders.

'Let's creep up on them,' Britta said.

'Yes,' Anna and I said. 'Let's creep up on them. We've got to find out what they're up to.'

When it was lunchtime we sat on our front steps and kept a lookout. All of a sudden Lasse appeared, and after a moment Bosse turned up. And a moment later, Olle. But they didn't all come from the same direction. Then we realized they had a secret and we weren't allowed to know what it was, otherwise they would all have turned up at the same time. We had our dolls with us on the steps so the boys wouldn't know we were spying on them. We played with the dolls and didn't say a thing to the boys. Then we all went and ate lunch. As soon as we had eaten we hurried back to the steps.

After a while Lasse came out. We played with the dolls. Lasse played with Milo sort of in passing, then suddenly sped around the corner of the house. We raced up to my room because we could see him from there through the window. He looked about warily and then ran straight through the currant bushes and jumped over the stone wall which runs round our garden. Then we couldn't see him any longer.

Soon Bosse followed after him. He walked slowly and calmly, and disappeared in the same direction as Lasse.

'You watch,' said Britta. 'It won't be long before Olle turns up. Quick, let's run down to the currant bushes and hide there!'

So we did. We crawled behind the bushes and sat in absolute silence, and in a little while Olle came running past. He ran so close to us that we could almost have touched him, but he didn't see us. We tiptoed after him.

Behind our garden is a big field. It is full of hazel bushes and juniper bushes and all sorts of other bushes. Trees, too. Dad says he is going to chop down all the bushes to make the field better for the cows to graze in, but I hope he doesn't because it is full of such good hiding places. We had sneaked after Olle for a long way when all of a sudden he jumped into some thick undergrowth and hey presto he was gone. We couldn't find him however hard we tried. We knew the boys were in the field and we looked high and low, but there was no sign of them. Then Anna said:

'I know, let's get Svipp! He'll find Olle.'

Britta and I thought that was a very good idea. We ran to South Farmhouse and asked Olle's mum if we could borrow Svipp for a little while.

'Yes of course you can,' she said. Svipp was so happy when he realized he was coming with us for a walk. He jumped up and barked. Then we said to him:

'Svipp, where's Olle? Find Olle!'

Svipp began to sniff the ground and all we had to do was follow after him. Straight across the currant patch he ran, and out into the field, with us running after. We raced like mad between the hazel bushes and then all of a sudden Svipp jumped right on top of Olle. Because there was Olle, with Bosse and Lasse standing beside him. And there was the secret, too. And the secret was a camp the boys had built in the field.

'Ha ha, you never expected that,' we said. And they hadn't.

'Don't try having any secrets from us,' we said. 'Because we'll find them all out one by one.'

'Only when you use a tracker dog to help you,' Lasse said.

Svipp jumped about and was happy, thinking he had done something very good. We told him he would have a big meaty bone for his dinner.

It was a brilliant camp the boys had built. They had nailed some planks around four trees like four corners of a square, with a tree in each corner. Then they had put juniper bushes all around to make the walls, because there weren't enough planks, Lasse said. And then they had laid small planks on top for a roof, and above that an old horse blanket.

'Do you think the girls can join in?' Lasse asked Bosse and Olle.

'Hmm, what do you think?' they said, because I expect they wanted to know what Lasse thought first. Lasse said we could join in.

So we played Indians in the camp. Lasse was the chief and he was called Strong Panther, and Bosse was Swift Deer and Olle was Flying Falk. Britta was given the name Growling Bear and Anna Yellow Wolf and me Sly Fox. I would have preferred a better name, but Lasse wouldn't let me. We didn't have a campfire but we pretended we had one, and we sat round it smoking the pipe of peace, which was a liquorice pipe. I bit off a tiny, tiny bit of the pipe of peace, and it tasted lovely.

The boys had made bows and arrows and they made some for us, too. Lasse said there were more Indians at the other end of the field. They were called Comanches and were sly and dangerous and we had to defeat all of them. We took our bows and arrows and rushed across the field with a terrifying cry.

Our cows were walking about at the far end of the field. Lasse said they were the Comanches. Oh, how those Comanches ran! Lasse shouted something at them in Indian language, but I don't think they understood.

WE GO BACK TO SCHOOL

When you have had a very long summer holiday, it's nice to go back to school again. At least, that's what I think. Bosse says he's going to write to the king and ask him to shut down all the schools, but I hope the king doesn't do that because I like school. I like our teacher and I like my school friends, and I like my school books when I have covered them in lovely new paper and stuck on labels with my name on. Lasse and Bosse don't cover their books in new paper, unless Mum or the teacher says they have to. And they make their books untidy too. Lasse cuts out the comic strip people from newspapers and sticks them in his geography book. He says it's more interesting that way, and I think he is probably right. If the sentence beneath a picture says 'Chinese farmer planting rice', most of the man looks Chinese but his head looks like the Phantom.

All of us Noisy Village children walk to school together. We have to leave home at seven o'clock because we have such a long way to go. We take milk and sandwiches with us, which we have at school in the morning break. Sometimes Lasse and Bosse and Olle eat theirs on the way, before we have even got to school.

'Why pack your packed lunch in your backpack when you can pack it in your stomach,' Lasse says.

Our teacher lives on the top floor of the schoolhouse. She has such a lovely room with a piano and lots of books and a dear little kitchen. We help carry in her logs. Sometimes she lets us borrow her books, and sometimes she makes us hot chocolate.

Once when we arrived at school, our teacher was ill, so there couldn't be any school that day.

All the other children apart from us Noisy Village children knew about it already, because there are telephones in Storby Village, but there are none in Noisy Village. We didn't know what to do when we found the schoolroom locked and no children and no teacher. Finally we went upstairs and knocked on our teacher's door.

'Come in,' she said.

So we went in. And there she lay, very ill. There should have been a woman coming to help her, but she hadn't arrived. So our teacher asked if we wanted to help her instead. And we did. The boys ran to get logs and Britta lit the fire and put on some water for tea. I swept the floor and shook her pillows, and Anna laid the tray. Then we served our teacher tea and sandwiches.

She said she had such a longing to eat stew for dinner, and she had the meat at home. She wondered if we could make the stew, if she told us how to do it.

'Well, we can try, Miss,' said Britta. 'And if it doesn't turn out to be stew perhaps it will turn out to be something else.'

But it did turn out to be stew, and now that I know how to make it I don't have to learn when I get older. Miss offered us some stew, and it was delicious. Afterwards Britta washed up and I dried up. Lasse and Bosse and Olle sat next to our teacher's bookcase and read all the time, because boys never do anything useful. We stayed with Miss until the end of the school day, and then we asked her if she was thinking of being ill the next day too, and she said she was. So we wondered if we could come and help her again. Miss said she would be very happy if we would like to do that.

When we got there next day, me and Britta and Anna, our teacher was lying in her bed and it was all untidy, and she was longing for porridge, poor thing. We helped her to sit in the rocking chair and then we made her bed so that it was lovely and smooth, and when she got back into bed she said she felt like a princess. Then we made porridge for her, and afterwards we made coffee and gave her fresh cinnamon buns that I had brought from home. That's when our teacher said it was very nice being ill. What a pity she was completely better the next day, otherwise we would have learned how to make even more meals.

In the autumn and the winter it is dark when we go to school in the morning and dark when we come home again in the afternoon. It wouldn't be very nice walking all alone in the dark, but because there are six of us we have lots of fun. We walk through forest almost all the way and Lasse tries to make us believe it is full of trolls and giants and witches. Perhaps it is, but we haven't seen any. Sometimes the stars are shining high up in the sky when we walk home. Lasse says there are two million, five hundred thousand and fifty-five stars in the sky, and he says he knows the name of each and every one. I think he's making that up because once I asked him the name of a star and he said it was called Lovelybigstar. But the next day, as we were walking home from school, I asked about the same star again, and that time he said it was called The Queen's Crown.

'No, yesterday you said it was called Lovelybigstar,' I said.

And then Lasse said:

'No, it wasn't that one! Lovelybigstar fell down during the night. That one is called The Queen's Crown. Honestly!'

Sometimes we sing on our way home from school. *I Love to Go A'Wandering*, and things like that. Imagine if anyone heard. Wouldn't they like to know who was singing! Because it is so dark they wouldn't be able to see that it is only us Noisy Village children, walking along in the darkness, singing.

WHEN WE DRESSED UP

One evening last autumn all the Noisy Village parents had gone to a party at the shopkeeper's in Storby Village. Only us children were at home. Oh, and Grandad, of course. And Agda. I flashed my torch three times at Britta and Anna through the window. That means: Come over immediately, I've got something to tell you!

It wasn't long before I heard them coming up the stairs. Actually, I didn't have anything to tell them, I only wanted us to think of something fun to do. First we looked at all my bookmarks and then we played

Ludo for a while. Then we thought we would go downstairs and talk to Agda. But that's when Anna had a really good idea. She thought we ought to dress up so Agda wouldn't recognize us. Oh, how we rushed about getting ready! There were masses of clothes belonging to Mum and Dad hanging on the landing. Britta said she was going to dress up as a man, so she took Dad's striped trousers and a brown jacket, and his round black hat, and put them on. The trouser legs were too long, of course, so she fastened them up with safety pins, and she had to roll up the sleeves as well. Then she drew a moustache and beard on her face. She looked like a funny little old man, and Anna and I laughed at her so much we could hardly get our skirts on. I had a black skirt that was Mum's, and a flowery blouse, and I put on a black hat with a veil. When I pulled the veil down over my face, Britta and Anna didn't recognize me. Anna also wanted a veil but we couldn't find any more, and no more hats either, so Anna had to tie a scarf over her head. She was also wearing a long skirt, with a woolly cardigan.

Lasse and Bosse were over at Olle's house, so we came downstairs without anyone seeing us. We tiptoed out through the front door and round to the kitchen door, and knocked. We knocked loudly.

'Who's there?' asked Agda from inside, and she sounded a bit afraid. At first we didn't know what to say, but then Britta answered in a deep voice:

'Tramps!'

'You can't come in here. They're not at home,' Agda said.

'We *want* to come in,' we shouted, banging on the door, but then we couldn't help laughing. I tried to laugh quietly, but the laughter was bubbling up so much inside me that I think Agda must have heard. Slowly she opened the door a crack and we barged in.

'Well, I never,' Agda said. 'Who are these fine people out for a stroll?'

'My name is Mr Karlsson,' Britta said. 'And these are my wives.'

'What stylish wives you have, Mr Karlsson,' Agda said. 'And two of them, as well. May I offer you ladies and gentleman something to drink?'

She most certainly could. We drank juice and pretended we were grown-ups, and it worked much better than usual, now that we were wearing grown-up clothes.

Then we thought we would go to South Farmhouse and show the boys. The front door wasn't locked, so we were able to walk right in. As we were going up the stairs to Olle's room on the top landing, Anna tripped on her long skirt and made such an awful noise that Olle came out to see what was happening. And do you know what? He was so scared that he actually jumped when he caught sight of us. It was dark on the landing and there was only a little bit of light coming from the door. I expect he thought we were three ghosts standing there at the top of the staircase.

When Lasse saw that we were dressed up, he wanted to dress up too, and so did Bosse and Olle. Lasse put on a dress which belonged to Olle's mum, and shoes with high heels. Bosse and Olle put on men's clothes. Lasse ran around flapping his arms and speaking in a squeaky voice.

'How *do* you make your ginger biscuits so delicious, my dear? Oh, *may* I have the recipe?'

He thinks that's how grown-up ladies speak.

Then we all went to say hello to Grandad, to tell him we were dressed up. It was very sad that he couldn't see it for himself. We made up a little play and acted for him for ages. In the play Lasse was an angry lady. Oh, how we laughed at him! Grandad laughed too, even though he couldn't see, but only hear.

THE GREAT SNOW STORM

Now I'm going to tell you about the great storm that came just before Christmas. It was the worst storm Dad had ever seen, he said.

Ever since the beginning of December Lasse had been saying every day on our way to school:

'There won't be any snow for Christmas, just you wait and see.'

It made me very sad every time he said that, because I really, really wanted there to be snow. But the days passed one by one without even the tiniest little snowflake. But guess what, in Christmas week, just as we were sitting in school doing sums, Bosse yelled:

'Look! It's snowing!'

And it was. We were so happy that we all shouted: 'Hooray!'

Our teacher said we should all stand up and sing *In the Deep Midwinter*.

When we went outside at break time there was a thin layer on the playground. We trampled a large figure of eight in the snow and ran round and round in it for the whole break, shouting at the top of our voices. But Lasse said:

'Well, this is all the snow we'll be getting.'

When we went to school the next day the snow was deep enough at least for us to have to trudge our way through it, and it was still snowing. But Lasse said:

'There won't be any more snow, and even this will melt before Christmas.'

That's what he thought. The very minute we walked through the school door the snow started falling heavily. It snowed until everything was completely white outside the window, and you couldn't even see across the playground. All day it carried on snowing, and the wind began blowing too. It blew and snowed, snowed and blew, until at last our teacher became anxious and said:

'I don't know how you Noisy Village children are going to get home today.'

She wondered if we would like to stay with her overnight, and we did really want to do that, but we knew how worried everyone in Noisy Village would be if we didn't come home. So we told her we couldn't stay, and that's when our teacher said it would be best if we set off for home straight away, before it got dark.

It was one o'clock when we left school. Oh, you should have seen the piles of snow! And it was blowing a gale! We had to almost bend double as we walked.

'Is this enough snow for you now?' Britta said crossly to Lasse.

'It's not Christmas yet,' he answered, but we could hardly hear what we were saying because of the wind.

We walked and walked and walked. We held each other's hands so that we wouldn't get separated. The snow reached way over my knees, and you don't walk very fast when that happens, I can tell you. The wind blew right through us and we became so cold that we lost all feeling in our toes and fingers and noses. Eventually my legs were so tired that I told Lasse I needed to rest for a while.

'Not on your life,' Lasse said. Anna was also tired and she wanted to rest as well, but Lasse said it was dangerous. Then Anna and I started to cry, because we thought we would never, ever, come home to Noisy Village again. We were only halfway by that time. Then all of a sudden Olle said:

'I know, we'll go to the shoemaker's! He can't bite off our noses, after all.'

Anna and I wanted to go to the shoemaker's even if he *did* bite off our noses.

The wind was so strong we practically blew straight in through the shoemaker's door. He didn't seem especially happy to see us.

'Kids have no business being out in such weather,' he said.

We didn't dare say that it hadn't been such weather when we left home that morning. We took off our outer clothes and sat down to watch as he hammered tacks into shoes. We were very hungry, but we didn't dare say that, either. The shoemaker made coffee for himself and ate a sandwich, but he didn't offer us anything. It wasn't the same as being with Kristin in Lövnäset during the thunderstorm.

When it started to get dark the snow and wind stopped, but there were such big snowdrifts we had no idea how we were going to be able to get home anyway. Oh, how I longed to be home in Noisy Village, for Mum, and for my bed.

Then guess what? All of a sudden we heard the sound of bells out in the snow, and we ran to the window to look. And there was Dad, coming along with the snowplough! We opened the door and shouted to him, even though the shoemaker said:

'Don't let all the cold air in!'

Dad was so happy when he saw us. He shouted that he was going to plough all the way to Storby Village and then collect us on the way back.

And he did. We were allowed to sit on the snowplough, me and Anna, and the others had to walk behind. The road was cleared now, of course, so it wasn't exactly difficult.

Mum was standing at the kitchen window looking very worried when we arrived home. Lasse and Bosse and I were given hot soup with dumplings, and it was the best thing I had ever tasted. I ate three bowls full. Afterwards I went to bed straight away, and that felt very nice. Mum said she'd had a feeling Dad ought to get out with the snowplough because she thought we had to be on the road somewhere. What a good job she had a feeling, otherwise we would have had to stay at the shoemaker's all night.

NEARLY CHRISTMAS

The next day the sun was shining and the snow lay so white and beautiful on all the trees. It was the last day of school before Christmas. Our teacher said she hadn't slept a wink all night. She had been lying awake, wondering whether we had managed to survive in all the snow, she said.

Because it was the last day before Christmas, Miss read a Christmas story to us. Everything felt so special somehow, and the very best thing of all happened just as we were about to leave for home. Our teacher had written to Stockholm and ordered storybooks for us. We had been shown a big poster with lots of pictures on it which were the front covers of books. We were allowed to choose which books we wanted to buy. I had chosen two and so had Lasse and Bosse. There were such beautiful princes and princesses on mine. And today, our last day of term, the books had arrived. Our teacher walked around, handing them out. I could hardly wait until I got mine, but Mum had said we mustn't read them until Christmas Eve.

Before we went home we sang all the Christmas songs we knew, and our teacher said that she hoped we would have a lovely Christmas. I knew I was going to.

Britta and Anna and I ran to the shop and bought shiny red and green and white and blue paper, because we were going to make paper baskets to hang on the Christmas tree. Then we went home. Everything was so light and beautiful.

As we were walking along Britta took out her storybook. She smelled it, and then we were all allowed to smell it. New books smell so nice that you can tell from the smell how much fun it will be to read them. Then Britta started to read. Her mum had also said that the books should be saved until Christmas Eve, but Britta said she was only going to read a tiny, tiny bit. When she had read that bit we all thought it was so awfully exciting that we told her she could read another tiny bit. So she read a bit more. But that didn't help because after she had finished it was just as exciting as before.

'I've simply *got* to know if someone put a spell on the prince or not,' said Lasse.

So she had to read a bit more, and we went on like that, until by the time we finally got home to Noisy Village she had read the whole book to us. Britta said it didn't matter, she was going to read it all again on Christmas Eve anyway.

Back at our house Mum and Agda were busy making Christmas sausages, and it was untidy everywhere. As soon as we had eaten, we went outside, Lasse, Bosse, and me, and built a lovely big snow lantern in the garden. Britta and Anna and Olle came to help.

There were loads of sparrows and bullfinches and blackbirds in the linden tree, and they looked so hungry that I ran to ask Dad if we could put out the Christmas sheaves for them a little earlier than usual. Dad said we could, so we all ran down to the barn and took the five sheaves of oats that had been put aside as Christmas sheaves during the threshing. We hung them in the apple tree in our garden, and it wasn't long before the birds were there, enjoying their food. They probably thought it was Christmas Eve already. It all looked so beautiful, the Christmas sheaves and the snow and everything.

In the evening Britta and Anna and I sat in Grandad's room making Christmas tree baskets. The boys were there too. At first they weren't going to help make any baskets, but then, after a while, they couldn't stop themselves after all. We all sat at Grandad's round table and we made fifty-four woven paper baskets, which we shared out equally, so there were eighteen baskets for North Farmhouse, eighteen for Middle Farmhouse, and eighteen for South Farmhouse. Grandad gave us apples and barley sugar to eat. All the time we were sitting there I was thinking about the gingerbread biscuits we were going to make the next day. It was almost as much fun as Christmas Eve.

In the middle of it all Lasse ran out into the garden and lit the candle we had put inside the snow lantern. Oh, how beautifully the snow lantern shone in the darkness! When I saw it shining out there in the garden, it made me think of that song, *Christmas is Waiting Outside our Snowy Door*. I could really imagine Christmas waiting there on the doorstep, glowing like the snow lantern.

'You poor thing, Grandad. You can't see the snow lantern,' Anna said. 'Shall we sing for you instead?' she asked, because Grandad likes to hear us singing very much. And so we did. We sang that very song I had been thinking of, *Christmas is Waiting*.

'Don't you think Christmas is fun,' whispered Anna to me afterwards. And I said I did. Because I do. I think Christmas is the best thing I know. All of us Noisy Village children have so much fun at Christmas.

Well, we have lots of fun at other times too, of course, summer and winter, and spring and autumn. Oh, what a lot of fun we have!

Astrid Lindgren

Astrid Lindgren was born in Vimmerby, Sweden in 1907. In the course of her life she wrote over 40 books for children, and has sold over 145 million copies worldwide. She once commented, 'I write to amuse the child within me, and can only hope that other children may have some fun that way too.'

Many of Astrid Lindgren's stories are based upon her memories of childhood and they are filled with lively and unconventional characters. Perhaps the best known is *Pippi Longstocking*, first published in Sweden in 1945. It was an immediate success, and was published in England in 1954.

Awards for Astrid Lindgren's writing include the prestigious Hans Christian Andersen Award. In 1989 a theme park dedicated to her—*Astrid Lindgren Värld* (Astrid Lindgren World)—was opened in Vimmerby. She died in 2002 at the age of 94.

Note on the text

The Children of Noisy Village was originally published in Swedish in 1947, titled *Alla vi barn I Bullerbyn*, and has been a much-loved tale in many countries around the world since then. The story is set in a particular time and place, and there may be some things which seem odd to us today. For example, when the story was written, collecting birds' eggs was a popular hobby. However, we now know that this is harmful and wrong, and is illegal in many countries including the UK and Sweden. Nevertheless, we hope that *The Children of Noisy Village* will continue to entertain and delight readers for many years to come.